Emmabella's Christmas Alphabet

E. E. Murray

Book A

For Alexander

Contents

Introduction 1

A is for Attic 4

B is for Basement 6

C is for Christmas, of course! 12

D is for Damn! 13

E is for Emmabella 16

F is for Fionton 23

G is for Giving 42

H is for Horrible Woodchip Wallpaper 43

I is for Injury 44

J is for Jesus 45

K is for Kraaack! 49

L is for Laugh 50

M is for Mum 51

N is for Noddy 52

O is for Obstetrics   56

P is for Patient   59

Q is for Question Mark   60

R is for Receiving   64

S is for Sprain (not a)   65

T is for Tip   66

U is for Understatement   68

V is for Virgo and Daughters   71

W is for World's Best Roast Potatoes   73

X is for X-ray   76

Y is for Yes   78

Z is for Zebra   79

Introduction

This is the story of my Christmas.

I love Christmas but this year's Christmas was a little bit different. There was a turkey and presents and crackers as usual but there were also tears, a tantrum, a gunfight, a broken ankle and the complete and utter destruction of my bedroom.

And a kettle.

The best way to put it is to say that this Christmas wasn't neatly ordered and arranged and I really like things to be neatly ordered and arranged. I also like things that make sense and for much of this Christmas, much of this Christmas didn't make sense.

I have thought a lot about the best way to tell my story; to tell you how very far away from neatly ordered and arranged this Christmas was and after much consideration I have decided to use the one thing I know that makes perfect sense.

The alphabet!

That's right, the alphabet. I'm going to tell you all about my last Christmas (not my last Christmas as in my last *ever* Christmas – my last Christmas as in the Christmas that has just gone) from A to Z.

The alphabet is the most neatly ordered and arranged thing in the world and the alphabet makes total sense. It contains all the letters we need to make all the words we need. How perfect is that? Without the alphabet, I wouldn't be able to write these words and you wouldn't be able to read them.

This is what my story would look like without the alphabet:

See? That just wouldn't work at all.

So what better way to tell you about my Christmas?

Of course, you'll want to know all about me and you will – at least as much as I'm willing to tell. For now, though, I need to begin in a neatly ordered and arranged way. And that means starting with:

A is for Attic

Dad was up in the attic looking for the Christmas decorations. I could hear him clattering about in the dark and dusty space above my bedroom.

I love my room and I've got it exactly how I want it. Everything is where it should be; everything is neatly ordered and arranged. I've got an old wooden wardrobe with a mirror on its door and two drawers. I always hang my clothes in the wardrobe or fold them neatly and put them away in the drawers. I never, ever leave my clothes lying around on the floor (unlike someone I know).

Against the wall across from my bed is my bookshelf containing my favourite books including a battered old dictionary (my favourite book of all) and next to the bookshelf is my desk where I do all my homework. On the desk is my laptop and a chipped coffee mug containing my pens (black, blue and red for corrections) and my pencils (all sharpened and all pointing upwards). Next to the mug is a stapler, a pencil sharpener, an eraser and a large black hole punch. I've never had a reason to use the hole punch but Dad brought it back from his office one day because they no longer needed it and it's stationery so I just couldn't say no.

Also on the desk is a Valentine's Day card. It is the first Valentine's Day card I have ever received and it has been sitting on my desk since February. Every time I clean my room (yes, I clean my own room, at least once a week) I lift it up to polish the desk. It's at this point that I look at the card and hope, hope, hope that it was sent by the only person I would ever want to send me a Valentine's Day card.

I think I know who sent it. At least I *think* I think I know who sent it.

These are the reasons why I think I know who sent it:

1) He looked at me and smiled the day before Valentine's Day.

2) I really, really hope it's him.

There, that should do it.

B is for Basement

That was where Mum was. She was looking for the Christmas decorations, too.

We moved into this house in January and anything that wasn't needed immediately was taken down to the basement or packed away in the attic. Dad was convinced that the decorations were in the attic and Mum was equally convinced that they were in the basement.

It's been a bit of an odd year. Moving into a new house was exciting but ever since then things have been a bit... I don't really know the right word to use (and I always like to use the right word)... a bit... different (that *isn't* the right word but it's the best I can do at the moment).

It feels a bit like Mum has spent the entire year in the basement and Dad has been up in the attic the whole time. Not literally, of course, that wouldn't work very well.

They have been talking because they have had to talk. Words sometimes come out of their mouths and sometimes seem to be directed at the other person. But two people talking doesn't mean they are having a conversation and it certainly doesn't mean that they are enjoying talking to the other person.

They have spent the whole year in separate rooms.

This is metaphor. A metaphor is when you describe something using words that actually describe something else. Like saying two people have spent the whole year in separate rooms when they haven't actually spent the whole year in separate rooms. What you are really trying to say is that they haven't been talking to each other in the way they used to talk to each other. At all.

At school our English teacher is called Mr French. Confusing, eh? To add to the confusion, our French teacher is called Miss English. Really. Once in French, Mark Dangerfield asked Miss English a question: 'Miss English,' he said, 'if you and Mr French got married and had children, what language would they speak?' Everyone else sniggered because they thought that Mark was being rude. Beyond rude, actually. But I didn't. I thought he was being bold and brave and daring. And magnificent. Miss English blushed a bit and moved on quickly. Anyway, Mr French (French equals English and English equals French, remember) is trying to get us all to use more metaphors in our written work.

In one class last term, we all had to pair up and write a description of our partner using metaphors. For some strange reason, I got paired up with Sophie Gallimore – worst, worst, worst luck. Whenever there is trouble in the playground it will almost always involve Sophie Gallimore or her twin brother Sam (or both). Penny Tupper, my sometimes best friend (long story…) says that Sophie is a girl of few words who prefers to let her hands and feet do the talking. She certainly used few words in Mr French's metaphor challenge. Here is what Sophie wrote about me:

She looks like a duck.

Short, to the point and completely wrong. True, my eyes could be bigger and less brown; my hair could be blonder and less mousey; my nose could be less pointy and my mouth could be less droopy at the sides but I certainly don't look like a duck.

I might look a bit like a goose (a goose with freckles) but not a duck.

Anyway, Sophie got no marks at all, which served her right. She hadn't put enough effort into it and she hadn't even used a metaphor. Sophie had used a simile. A simile is a bit like a metaphor except you use the words 'as' and 'like' to make a comparison between two things. 'The apple is as a green as a cucumber' is a simile. So is 'Sophie Gallimore is as mean as measles.'

Everyone else wrote rude things about everyone else, too. Everyone except me and after seeing what Sophie had written I was a bit sad that I hadn't.

The whole task caused a lot of upset and arguments which continued for the rest of the lesson and spilled out into the playground at break time. English is my favourite lesson and I really like Mr French but I don't think he'd thought this through properly.

So Mum was in the basement and Dad was in the attic and they were both looking for the Christmas decorations. And it was Christmas Eve. This isn't a metaphor or a simile, this is a fact. I had opened the last window on my advent calendar that morning – it was definitely Christmas Eve.

You may be asking yourself why we had left it until Christmas Eve to put up our decorations. Well, Dad had been away with his work (he's a surveyor and is often away surveying things) and Mum said that we all had to put the decorations up together because that is what we always did (she stressed that it was *particularly* important that we did this *this* year); it is a tradition. Mum says that Christmas is a time for traditions. This is also a fact as we don't seem to have traditions at any other time of the year.

By the way, Mum and Dad don't call the basement a basement, they call it a cellar. I call it a basement because I probably watch too many American films. And anyway, I couldn't have written 'C is for Cellar', because...

C is for Christmas, of course!

My favourite time of the year. This year everyone was coming to us for Christmas Day. By 'everyone' I mean Nana and Grandpa Grundy (Mum's mum and dad), Auntie Maisie (Mum's sister) and Uncle Dougie (Maisie's husband).

D is for Damn!

That's what Dad said when he found out everyone was coming to us for Christmas Day.

Dad likes Auntie Maisie (Mum says he has a soft spot for her) and he likes Nana and Grandpa Grundy. But he never seems to see eye to eye with Uncle Dougie.

Uncle Dougie likes to talk a lot but he never has much to say to me except for when we play Monopoly at Christmas. Then, he's more than happy to taunt me for my Monopoly-playing mistakes, as he sees them. Mistakes like buying Old Kent Road, for instance. I get the impression he doesn't think there is much to be gained by talking to children so he just doesn't bother.

He always has plenty to say to Dad, though. Things like:

'Just the two pay rises for me this year...'

And:

'Are you still driving that old thing, Harvey? Come and look at this. New company car; walnut and leather trim, state of the art satnav, full Bluetooth connectivity, sixteen speakers...'

Occasionally he'll break off from telling Dad about his new car or latest achievements to answer his mobile phone (his mobile is never, ever switched off). When this happens he barks things about sales figures and optimum unit price margins down the phone.

I used to think Uncle Dougie was very important because he always has a nice car and his phone is always ringing. But he's not, really. He's a Regional Sales Manager, or something.

Uncle Dougie always dresses very smartly and his hair is always smooth and shiny. So is his face, now I think about it. He always smells of aftershave.

I don't think Auntie Maisie owns a hairbrush but she has more important things on her mind like climate change and the fate of the whales. She volunteers at the local hospice shop and once spent a week up a tree in a failed attempt to stop the Council from chopping it down.

Twice now I've secretly overheard Dad say to Mum that he doesn't know what Maisie sees in Dougie (a long time ago when they actually used to talk properly). Both times Mum replied that Maisie was the yin to Dougie's yang. I have no idea what this means.

E is for Emmabella

That's me! Emmabella Murray. Hall Monitor at St Chad's Middle School; Library Monitor at the same; loyal daughter of a mother and father; sister to an annoying brother and I shall have my vengeance in this life or the next! Mark Dangerfield has been saying something similar to this in the playground for weeks now and I think it sounds good. I have no idea what this means, either, or where Mark got it from; perhaps he just made it up. It sounds clever and mysterious so I'm guessing that he did.

There are lots of things I don't understand. It's a bit like the 'Art Club Incident'. Every Thursday after school I go to Art Club. At breakfast on the day of the first Art Club I had the following conversation with Dad:

Me: 'I'm going to Art Club after school.'

Dad: 'That sounds good. What's the first rule of Art Club?'

Me: 'I don't know. I've never been before.'

Dad: 'The first rule of Art Club is – you don't talk about Art Club.'

He laughed to himself as if it was a private joke. I suppose it actually was a private joke because I was the only other person there and I hadn't got a clue what he was talking about. I didn't ask him what he meant and he was wrong, anyway. There don't seem to be any rules at all. Mr Wise, our art teacher, expects us all to be quiet when we're working but that is more of a guideline than a rule, I think. Art Club is really interesting and I really enjoy it but I've never talked to Dad about it since.

Life can be confusing sometimes. I know I probably should have asked Dad what he meant but I didn't know whether he'd assumed I'd know what he was talking about or whether it actually was just a private joke. I think that's why I like things to be neatly ordered and arranged; it reduces the risk of possible confusion. It doesn't really work for conversations, though. They often turn out to be surprisingly confusing.

There's one thing I like almost as much as having things neatly ordered and arranged and that's words that rhyme.

In English we've been learning about poetry. We have been reading modern poems which don't rhyme and are quite boring and old poems which do rhyme and are much better. Here's a bit of one of my favourite poems:

> Tyger! Tyger! burning bright
> In the forests of the night.

See? That's by somebody called William Blake and even though he didn't know how to spell tiger (if Mr French had been marking his work he'd have put a red 'sp' next to 'tyger' - twice) he could certainly write an impressive rhyme.

Here's part of another poem that I like:

> In a coign of the cliff between
> lowland and highland,
> At the sea-down's edge
> between windward and lea,
> Walled round with rocks as an
> inland island,

The ghost of a garden fronts
the sea.

That's the first bit of a poem called *A Forsaken Garden* by Algernon (Algernon!) Charles Swinburne and just like the William Blake poem, it has a lovely rhyme. I don't know exactly what it means but I have a sneaking feeling that Algernon's poem might be about something other than a garden. I still read it from time to time and recite it in my head but it no longer makes me think of a ghost of a garden and it no longer makes me wonder what Algernon might have been trying to say when he wrote about the ghost of a garden; it makes me think about how Mum and Dad act when they are together.

It's good that I'm called Emmabella and it's good that I like words that rhyme because when I grow up and I'm going to be... drum roll, please... a writer! The entire world will know of Emmabella the Storyteller. I'm going to write stories that everyone will want to read - I'm going to be the world's greatest storyteller! Whenever anyone introduces me to someone else (at a party to celebrate my latest bestselling book, probably) they will be able to say, '...and this is Emmabella, the world's greatest storyteller!' or just, '...meet Emmabella *the* storyteller!' Yes, that's much better.

I'm going to write poems, too. Poems that rhyme.

I haven't actually done anything about becoming the world's greatest storyteller yet but I'm convinced it's going to happen. I've tried sitting at my desk and just writing but I never seem to know where to start. I think I probably need a push in the right direction to get me going.

There is a local author called Mr Coe who runs a weekly creative writing course for ten and eleven-year-olds. According to the local paper, he firmly believes that all children should be encouraged to write and write well and that's why he runs his courses. Unfortunately, and despite him saying in the paper that he believed *all* children should be given the opportunity to write well, he only ever takes on five pupils at a time. He is very, very strict on this point. Apparently, he's very strict about everything according to Penny Tupper who *is* one of Mr Coe's lucky five. Mum and Dad didn't sign me up quickly enough so I missed out. It was, perhaps not surprisingly, a communication problem between the two of them; each thought the other had contacted Mr Coe but neither asked the other if they'd actually done it. Neither of them had. I'm now on Mr Coe's reserve list, apparently.

I decided to make a New Year's resolution right then – even though it wasn't New Year yet. My resolution was this: I'm going to join Mr Coe's writing class.

How? No idea.

When? Soon... soonish... as soon as possible.

Somehow, somehow, somehow. It just must happen. And if it does, I am convinced that next year is going to be a really good year. Or at least better than this year which wouldn't be all that difficult.

I know my name is unusual because nobody else in the whole school is called Emmabella. Mum said that she let Dad go down to the Council office on his own to register my name (she'd already done all the hard work, she said). I was supposed to be called Catherine but at that last minute Dad had a change of heart so I'm called Emmabella. It's an old family name, apparently (I had no idea who this family might be – I was fairly sure it wasn't ours).

Dad thinks it is a beautiful name and so do I.

My middle name is Edith which actually is a family name. Nana Grundy's first name is Edith although everyone who doesn't call her Nana calls her Edie.

Mum doesn't call me Emmabella. She calls me Emma.

F is for Fionton

Fionton is my younger brother and he makes me say 'Damn!' a lot even though I'm not supposed to. Sometimes I say it silently so that I'm the only one who knows that I'm saying it. Sometimes I say it under my breath hoping that I'm the only one who can hear what I'm saying. And sometimes I just can't help myself and I say it really, really loudly. Just like Dad did when he heard that everyone was coming to us for Christmas Day.

Dad was in charge of naming Fionton, too (Mum had done all the hard work again). It's pronounced 'Finton' and at first Mum thought that it was a spelling mistake, but it's not. Lots of Mum and Dad's friends did make spelling mistakes on the 'New Baby' cards they sent just after Fionton was born, though. Years later Mum told me that there were lots of Fintons, Fintens and at least one Phinton.

Nana Grundy was the only one to get it right.

The way his name is spelt doesn't actually matter that much; everyone calls him Finn. Apart from Mum who calls him Fionton when she's cross with him. She calls him Fionton a lot and says 'Damn!' in the same sentence quite a lot, too.

Mum also says that a problem shared is a problem halved. I'm not entirely sure about this. What if I have a problem (say, for example, I'm worried that my parents aren't talking to each other) and then tell someone else. Does that really mean that my problem is halved? And if it does, haven't I just given half of my problem to someone else? That doesn't sound very fair. Or what if, when I'm telling someone else, I miss out something important? I might only pass on a quarter of the problem leaving me with three quarters of the problem; that wouldn't halve my problem at all.

It's all very confusing.

Anyway, my worries about Mum and Dad were stuck in my mind – stuck fast, in fact – and no matter how hard I tried to forget them or make them seem less important by thinking about nice things like my dictionary or Mark Dangerfield they just wouldn't go away. So I slowly came round to the idea that talking to somebody about my worries might actually help.

But who to talk to?

Certainly not Penny Tupper and certainly not Molly Moon (my other sometimes best friend – even longer story). Their homes and their lives are so perfectly perfect that I didn't think I'd get much in the way of understanding from them. I certainly couldn't talk to Mark Dangerfield (more's the pity) because... well, just because.

So I decided to talk to Finn.

Yes, yes, I know. He's my younger brother and he makes me say 'Damn!' a lot and in the normal scheme of things I'm not supposed to get on with him, never mind confide in him and discuss my worries and concerns with him. But the truth is I don't dislike Finn – just the opposite, actually. He is annoying, we don't always get on, but he's my brother and, well, I love him, really.

So one afternoon in September (see how long I held on to my worries all by myself - this all started way back at the beginning of the year) I went looking for Finn in his room.

You'd think a nine-year-old boy would be easy to find in a normal-sized bedroom, wouldn't you? Well, he wasn't.

Discarded clothes fought for floor space with teetering piles of books and three traffic cones. There was an old wind-up gramophone from Grandpa Grundy on a low table and an old valve radio, also from Grandpa, in various pieces at the foot of the bed.

A bright orange piece of fabric (an Indian design, I think) hung on one wall and on another was a massive map of the world. The map had various brightly coloured pins stuck in it at seemingly strategic locations. I had no idea what the significance of these pins was but it wouldn't surprise me if Finn was planning some form of world domination in the future.

In a dusty corner next to the bed was Finn's collection of brightly-painted magic wands. He'd spent much of the previous summer making these wands out of twigs, chopsticks and any other wand-like materials he could lay his hands on. He even made one for me.

I tested it by pointing it at my Valentine's Day card and shouting 'Abracadabra!' in the hope that it might shed some light on who'd given it to me. It didn't. I told Finn that his magic wand didn't work, to which he replied, 'They work all right. But you have to have 'The Power'. You obviously haven't got it.'

On a low table under the map of the world was Finn's Venus flytrap. I don't know where Venus flytraps come from – I know where *this* Venus flytrap came from, it was a birthday present from Auntie Maisie a couple of years ago – I mean don't know where in the world they come from. I'm guessing it's somewhere exotic and hot which makes me wonder how Finn manages to keep his growing. We have a few flies zooming around in the summer but none in the winter and I know it needs flies to survive. I thought it would wilt and die in the winter like the sunflowers I used to grow at our old house, but it didn't. It's just grows bigger and bigger.

It was Finn's mess of blonde hair that I saw first through the rib cage of a life-size skeleton hanging from its purpose-built stand. The skeleton is a plastic replica, apparently. I hope so. He was at his desk putting the finishing touches to a papier-mâché volcano he'd made. It was impressive, too (damn, damn, damn him – clever *and* talented).

Anyway, this is how the conversation went:

Me: 'All right?'

Finn: 'Fine. You?'

Me: 'Fine. Fine-ish. Actually, not all that fine. Actually.'

Finn: 'What's up?'

Me: 'Have you noticed anything funny about Mum and Dad?'

Finn: 'No.'

Me: 'Oh. Okay then.'

Finn: 'Is that it then?'

Me: 'Yes.'

Finn: 'Okay then.'

This wasn't getting me anywhere and I still had 100% of my problem. I tried changing the subject.

'You know your Venus flytrap,' I said.

He pointed at his Venus flytrap. 'That Venus flytrap?'

'Have you got another one?' I asked.

He shook his head.

'Then yes. That Venus flytrap.'

'Yeah, I know it.'

'How come it grows so well even in winter?'

He just gave me a smug look and tapped his nose with his index finger.

By way of a reply, I stuck my tongue out and meant it.

As we talked Finn carefully placed a glass tumbler into the crater of the volcano – he'd moulded the shape exactly so that the tumbler fitted perfectly. He filled the tumbler with cola and said, 'Watch this...'

He dropped two of the fizzy tablets Dad takes whenever he has an upset stomach into the cola-filled tumbler.

The effect was instant and staggering. The cola fizzed up like a foamy sea and bubbled over the lip of the volcano's crater before running, in lava-like streams, down the sides of the volcano. I was amazed.

'Pretty good, eh?' said Finn.

I was sure that it was. I was also sure that I had picked entirely the wrong time to talk to him about my concerns about Mum and Dad.

As the volcanic eruption subsided Finn began to wipe up the cola with one of his T-shirts and I, somehow, managed to find a space on his bed to sit down. Looking over at his large wall map, I tried to see if I could work out some scheme behind Finn's positioning of the pins.

The first pinned place I saw was Edinburgh in Scotland and to the left of that Reykjavik in Iceland. Looking further down the map I saw that Florence in Italy and a small island called Skiathos in the Mediterranean Sea were also pinned.

There must have been about fifteen pins in total.

What did they all mean?

Scanning the whole world, I couldn't make out any particular pattern to the positions of the pins. Perhaps it was an anagram, I thought. Perhaps I needed to take the first letters of all the pinned places and rearrange them to spell out some secret message Finn had cunningly tried to hide.

I stood up to take a closer look and noticed that a place called Manila in the Philippines was pinned-

'What are you doing?' asked Finn sharply, still at his desk and with his back to me.

'Nothing,' I replied, quietly.

He'd cleaned up the cola and was now repeating his volcano experiment with lemonade (same result, different coloured lava).

Impressive as Finn's volcano was, I did what I should have done to begin with. I went to see Grandpa Grundy.

Grandpa Grundy was old and wise and could always be relied on to give good advice. I knew he would be on his own because it was a Saturday afternoon and Nana Grundy always plays Texas Hold 'Em (a poker game) with some friends of hers on Saturday. Grandpa Grundy likes to stay in and listen to sport on the radio on Saturday afternoons but I knew he would make time for me (he's kind like that).

By the way, a few years ago (I was five and Finn was four) Nana Grundy was babysitting us when Mum and Dad were out and she decided to teach me and Finn how to play Texas Hold 'Em. We both picked it up quickly and Finn proved himself to be quite a decent player. I, on the other hand, was useless. I just don't have a poker face and Nana Grundy could read me like a book (a book called *How to Win Money off Small Children*... Still, she'd given us the money to play with so it was probably only fair).

A few weeks after this, Mum and Dad had been at Finn's first parents' evening

(Finn had only started at First School at the beginning of that term) where they'd met his teacher who was a bit puzzled by one of the answers Finn had given in class. Apparently, they had been practising their counting when the teacher had asked if anyone knew what came after ten. Finn had eagerly raised his hand and said, 'Jack, Queen, King and Ace. Ace is high and you can't go round the corner to two.'

Mum and Dad had no idea where he had got this from.

Anyway, back to September and my worries...

I followed Grandpa through to his kitchen where he turned off the radio and we had the same conversation we always have whenever I visited him on a Saturday afternoon.

'How do you like your tea, Grandpa?'

'Made by somebody else,' he cheerfully replied.

It wasn't that he was lazy – anything but. He just truly believed that tea tasted better if it was made by somebody else (it certainly *did* taste better if it was made by me).

'Now,' he said as I passed him his cup of tea, 'what's on your mind?'

I just blurted it all out. I told him about Mum and Dad not talking, about how they hadn't been talking for a long time and about how I was worried about what might happen in the future.

'All right, Emma, just calm down,' he said. 'I can tell you not to worry and I can tell you that everything will be all right in the end because I am sure that it will be.'

'Are you certain?' I asked.

'I'm sure.'

'Why are you sure?'

'Emmabella, on their wedding day I gave your mother away. It was the happiest I had ever seen her. She was happy because she was marrying your father and she knew that she was doing the right thing. It was the right thing then and it's the right thing now.'

'Do you know what the problem is?' I asked.

Grandpa Grundy never liked to say the word 'no' even when 'no' was the right answer. He usually found some other way of saying of it.

'I'm quite sure I don't. Do you?'

I'd given this a lot of thought and I hadn't really been able to come up with anything. I know Dad likes to think that he is funny and he can be, but sometimes he says things without thinking. As Nana Grundy says, 'There's a time and a place' and I'm not sure that Dad always picks the right time. Or the right place, for that matter.

Earlier this year, for example, Mum and Auntie Maisie had gone on a diet together to encourage each other along. It had worked, too. They'd both lost a bit of weight but they'd been hungry all the time. One day, Dad came back from work to find Mum and Auntie Maisie in the kitchen and said, 'Here they are, The Hunger Dames!' If he was hoping to get a laugh, it didn't work (Finn laughed but he'd laugh at anything) and if he was hoping to break the ice with Mum it certainly didn't work.

I knew it wasn't that particular thing because they hadn't been talking for a long time before that. Perhaps Dad had said something else, before that, and that had been the cause of the trouble.

I only had one other idea but even I thought it was a bit silly.

'What is it?' asked Grandpa.

'You know how Nana says it's bad luck to put new shoes on a table?'

'I do. She's superstitious.'

'Are you superstitious, Grandpa?'

'I wouldn't say that.'

'Well,' I said, 'Just after we moved to the new house Dad bought a new pair of slippers-'

'Slippers aren't shoes.'

'But they're footwear.'

'Very true. Did your father put them on the table?'

'Yes! Well, sort of...'

'What does that mean?'

'He put them on the worktop in the kitchen.'

'So your father put something that isn't actually a shoe on something that isn't actually a table?'

'That's it, yes.'

'I think we can safely conclude that it's not that.'

'But that's all I can think of. I've no idea otherwise.'

'Then that is as it should be. There are some things, Emmabella, which we are not meant to know.'

'But if I knew what it was,' I protested, 'I might not be so worried.'

'Perhaps,' he replied. 'On the other hand, if you knew what it was you might be more worried.' He chuckled a little at this. I wasn't sure why.

'How serious do you think it is?'

Grandpa Grundy answered my question without really answering my question in much the same way as he says 'no' without actually saying 'no'.

'Lots of marriages go through choppy waters,' Grandpa Grundy had been in the navy. 'It can't all be plain sailing,' see?

'And I'm sure that soon enough all will be shipshape and Bristol fashion.' Told you.

'Is there anything I can do?'

'Not really. There is no magic wand. Be patient. These things take time. And *don't* worry.'

'Okay, Grandpa.'

'I mean it.'

'I'll really, really try.'

'See that you do. Now, can I put the radio back on? Derby are playing Middlesbrough and I'm missing it.'

I left Grandpa to his football and walked home through the small town that I had lived in all my life. I kept my head down as I plodded along the busy High Street; I didn't want to see anyone I knew. I just wanted to be alone.

Did I feel better for having talked to Grandpa? A little bit, I think, but I certainly didn't feel like my problem had been halved.

Grandpa was right about one thing, though. There are some things we aren't meant to know. Mum and Dad have no idea that every time Nana Grundy babysits me and Finn the three of us sit at the kitchen table and play Texas Hold 'Em. To be honest, my card skills haven't developed very much in all the years we've been playing but Finn has turned out to be a demon poker player.

At the end of the High Street the traders were packing up their stalls in the Market Place. It was busy and noisy as they called to each other and threw boxes into the backs of their vans so I hurried on until I found myself outside the Abbey.

The Abbey is the town's oldest and biggest building and it usually amazed and scared me at the same time. But it was different on that Saturday afternoon in September. Then, in the cool shadows of its towering walls, I felt a brief moment of calm as the shouts and bangs and clangs on the Market Place across the road completely faded away. The Abbey, oddly, felt like a warm embrace.

It wasn't really warm, of course, as I discovered when I reached out to touch one of the huge stones that made up the wall in front of me.

We'd learned about the Abbey at First School and that's how I knew that the rough stone my hand was pressed against had been placed in that spot over 800 years ago. Whose hands had put it there, I wondered. If the Abbey had a memory, would it be able to remember the person's name? Probably not after 800 years. It might still remember Mum and Dad's wedding, though; that was only fifteen years ago.

I left the warm embrace of the Abbey's cool shadows and headed home through the park. I followed the path that circled the bandstand where, as far as I knew, no band had ever played and then climbed the small hill beyond the swings and the slides (lots of children were playing there).

At the top of the slope I turned and saw the whole town spread out before me. It was more than just a town, I thought; it was my whole life.

In the distance to the right of the Abbey was the hospital where I had been born. To the left I could see my First School and beyond that St Chad's Middle School. I also saw my future in the shape of the High School way off on the edge of town. That's where Mum works and that's where I'll be going when I finish Middle School.

What else could I see? Was the house that I end up living in out there somewhere? Could I see the window of the room where I'll write my stories? Perhaps I won't be a writer at all and I'll teach in one of the schools or be a doctor or a nurse at the hospital.

Or perhaps I'll run away from this small town; just grab a bag and keep going until I find somewhere I'd like to live. Somewhere warm by the sea where I'll sleep in a hammock and live on oranges that'll wash up on the beach just when I need them.

This wasn't helping. I didn't want to think about my future and I certainly didn't want to
think about the past. I didn't want to think at all. But that is one of the hardest things to ever try to do.

G is for Giving

Nana Grundy says that it is better to give than to receive. I know she means well but I'm not absolutely convinced she's right. Especially at Christmas.

H is for Horrible Woodchip Wallpaper

That's what Mum calls it: 'Horrible woodchip wallpaper'. Do you know this stuff? It's just like normal wallpaper except it has bobbly bits in it. Mum says it was popular in the 1970s. It was everywhere when we moved here so Mum and Dad hired a machine called a wallpaper stripper from a Do It Yourself shop in town. Dad spent a week at Easter stripping all the old horrible woodchip wallpaper off the walls. He also ended up taking a lot of the plaster off the walls, too. They had to get a man in (a man who knew what he was doing, according to Mum) to re-plaster the walls and make them better again.

Dad forgot to strip the wallpaper off my bedroom ceiling. So now, thanks to the man who knew what he was doing, all the walls and ceilings in our house are perfectly smooth. Except for the ceiling in my bedroom which is still covered in horrible woodchip wallpaper.

I is for Injury

That's what Dad suffered when he fell through my bedroom ceiling from the attic. In between the shrieks of pain and wails of agony he was groaning something about slipping on one of the roof beams. From what I could make out, when you're in an attic you need to keep on the roof beams because they are strong and sturdy, the spaces in between the beams are not strong and sturdy at all. Dad hadn't stayed on the beams and that was why he now lay in a crumpled heap on my bedroom floor.

J is for Jesus

Christmas Day is the day that we celebrate Jesus' birth. In our house, we celebrate by giving and receiving presents. Finn and I save up a little of our pocket money and buy something for Mum (anything smelly that can be poured in the bath always seems to be appreciated. Mum says it helps her to relax) and something for Dad (socks or handkerchiefs always go down well. He always smiles and says thank you after he's opened them, anyway). We also get a box of chocolates for Nana and Grandpa Grundy. In return for our giving, we receive loads of presents so the system seems to work well.

This year Finn was hoping to get a Mega Blaster Laser Gun Set. This consists of two laser guns and two chest plates – it's a toy for two people. Each player straps on a chest plate and then they both chase each other around trying to shoot the plates with the laser guns (the plates make an electronic squeal when they receive a direct hit). And that's it. Finn thought that I would be happy to play Mega Blaster Laser Gun with him if he got it for Christmas. I thought Finn should prepare himself for disappointment.

There were some things I wanted for Christmas, too. Just little things, mostly, and one large and important thing. It's not as large and important as world peace (and everybody wants that, anyway) but it was important to me. It's a bit difficult to describe. I suppose I just wanted everything to be normal and I just wanted everyone to be happy.

When I put it like that, it doesn't really sound like a lot to ask, does it?

We also have a big meal of turkey and sausages wrapped in bacon and vegetables sometime on Christmas Day afternoon (or, as has happened on more than one occasion, in the early evening). Dad likes to make Christmas lunch and it is, as he says every year, a 'movable feast'. Usually when Dad is busy making lunch,

Mum likes to drink sweet sherry and giggle.

I don't know how anyone knows that the 25th of December was actually the day that Jesus was born. Finn was born on May the 6th nine years ago (one year and one week after me) and I try to forget his birthday every year. Not that I get much of a chance to forget it. He constantly reminds me because it's all he can talk about in the weeks leading up to it.

Jesus was born over 2,000 years ago so that's a lot of remembering. Perhaps it is just one of those things I'm not meant to understand like gravity (absolutely no idea...) and those hand soap dispenser things that Mum is so keen on (you press the nozzle down and the soap comes up. How does that even happen? As Nana Grundy would say, 'It's the devil's work, Emmabella, it's the devil's work.' And you know what? She's right). Anyway, I'm glad we remember Jesus' birthday and I'm glad that we celebrate.

'Jesus!' is also what Dad screamed out when he fell through my bedroom ceiling (sorry Jesus). I was lying on my bed reading a book at the time and that's definitely what he said. Hearing Dad scream 'Jesus!' was a bit of a surprise. It had also been a surprise to see him falling – suddenly and very, very quickly - from the ceiling on to my floor.

K is for Kraaack!

That was the sound I heard (complete with a capital 'K' – definitely not a 'C' - and an exclamation mark) when Dad hit the floor.

L is for Laugh

That's what Finn did when, having heard the commotion, he came rushing into my room and saw the huge, gaping hole in my ceiling. I thought he might have stopped laughing when he saw Dad writhing in agony on my bedroom floor but he didn't. If anything, he laughed more loudly.

I'm sure Dad would have told him off for being so badly behaved but he was still rolling around and wailing so he probably had more important things on his mind.

M is for Mum

Mum came rushing in just after Finn. She had heard the commotion, too (all the way from the basement!) and arrived in my room out of breath and in a flap. Unlike Finn, Mum didn't laugh when she saw Dad. She knew it was serious because she's a sensible adult (except when she's been at the sweet sherry on Christmas Day) and they know about these things.

After taking in the scene of devastation that was now my bedroom, Mum instinctively knew what to do. She tried to help Dad get back on his feet.

The conversation went like this:

Mum: 'Come on, let me help you up.'

Dad: 'Aaaagh!'

Mum: 'Which leg hurts?'

Dad: 'Aaaaaaaagh!'

Mum: 'Try putting your weight on your good leg.'

Dad: 'Aaaaaaaaaaaaaaaagh!'

N is for Noddy

Our next door neighbour is called Mr Oddy. His first name is Nigel and that's why Dad calls him 'Noddy'. Not to his face, of course, because that would be rude. I suppose Dad thought he would be on safe ground calling him 'Noddy' in front of me and Finn.

He wasn't.

The very next day we saw Mr Oddy fussing over the bedding plants in his front garden as we set off for school. Finn said:

'Morning, Noddy!'

Mr Oddy gave Finn a look (the sort of look that Mum describes as 'withering') and said:

'Yes, yes, very clever,' he then picked up his trowel, did a smart turn and headed back into his house.

Mr Oddy has had a difficult year, too. Mrs Oddy, who we never really knew, left him in January. Since then he's mooched around in a fog of gloom and despair like a (simile alert) single dark cloud in a blue sky. I quite like that. I might tell it to Mr French when we get back after the holiday. I'll change the names, of course. To protect the innocent. And the guilty.

Mr Oddy helped Mum carry Dad down the stairs, out of the house to the car.

Dad was no longer screaming and wailing. He was whimpering quietly and breathing quickly.

Mum was multitasking. She was helping to transport Dad out of the house *and* she was keeping a close eye on Finn. Mum was well aware of Finn's capacity to annoy other people and she'd also heard about the 'Noddy Incident' in the front garden (from Mr Oddy himself) so, as she and Mr Oddy carried Dad's limp body towards the car, she kept a watchful eye on him.

Whenever it looked like Finn was about to speak Mum shot him a look. It wasn't a withering look, though. It was a look that said: 'We are already having a bad day. Your father has hurt himself, there is a huge hole in your sister's ceiling, it is Christmas Eve and we still haven't found the decorations. We now have to go to the hospital to get your father treated and that will, no doubt, take the rest of the day. So don't toy with me, Buster. Don't even think about opening your mouth and trying to say something clever or funny. Now is not the time. Got it?' That was the gist of the look, anyway.

Surprisingly and to his credit, it looked as if Finn actually *had* got it. He was, as Nana Grundy might say, 'as quiet as the grave'. Well, almost...

The front passenger seat was pushed back as far as it would go to give Dad as much room as possible (deep and deliberate breaths and low moaning sounds at this point) which meant that I, in the seat behind him, had no room at all.

With my knees tucked up under my chin, Mum started the car and we set off for the hospital. As we pulled away from the kerb, Finn lowered his window and shouted to Mr Oddy:

'Thanks, Noddy!'

To take my mind off my crushed up legs which were getting sorer by the minute as we drove carefully (meaning very, very slowly) to the hospital, I thought about Finn. He was certainly cheeky for calling Mr Oddy 'Noddy' again. He knows, I think, the difference between right and wrong and he knows that words have consequences. Perhaps he just isn't bothered about the consequences. I sometimes think Finn must have a button in his brain – a button labelled MAYHEM that he can press at any time.

If I had a similar button in my head it would probably be labelled TIDY.

O is for Obstetrics

I like words and I like learning new words. At the hospital, on the way to the Accident and Emergency Department (Dad was now in a wheelchair that we had picked up in the reception area, being pushed along by Mum) we passed a sign pointing down a long corridor that said: 'Obstetrics'.

I paused for a moment because it looked like an interesting word and it was certainly new to me. I did what I always do with new words. I broke it down into smaller sections to make it easier for me to learn how to pronounce it properly:

OB

STET

RICS

I kept saying it, 'Ob...stet...rics,' as I hurried along the corridor to catch up with the others. 'Ob...stet...rics, ob...stet...rics, ob...stet...rics, obstetrics! Yes!'

We had a long wait at the Accident and Emergency Department but at least Dad wasn't screaming or wailing or whimpering or moaning anymore. He just had an agonised look on his face.

Eventually, a worn out looking woman in a white coat came along and wheeled Dad into one of the side rooms. Mum followed them in and came back out with the wheelchair a few minutes later.

'They're seeing to him now,' she said.

Finn and I knew this but it was nice to have the confirmation, anyway.

'Mum,' I said, 'what is obstetrics?'

'Obstetrics is where you go when you are having a baby,' she said.

'So Dad won't need to go there?' I said, trying to make conversation.

Mum laughed. 'No Emma, your father isn't having a baby,' she paused for a moment, 'he's just having kittens.'

She laughed at what I took to be a joke. I didn't laugh because I didn't get it.

'Don't worry,' she said, smoothing my hair, 'I'm sure it's just a sprain. He'll be up and about in no time.'

Clearly she thought that I was worried about Dad. I wasn't though. I was learning lots of new words like 'Obstetrics' and 'Radiography' and 'Ophthalmology' and 'Genito-urinary medicine'.

Finn wasn't worried either. He was perfecting handbrake turns in Dad's wheelchair.

I also knew that Dad's injury wasn't a sprain. Last year Penny Tupper sprained her ankle playing netball and earlier this year Finn sprained his ankle sliding down the stairs on an old metal tea tray. I witnessed both of these injuries and neither of them made any noise at all and most definitely not the sort of noise I heard when Dad hit my bedroom floor (see 'K' above).

P is for Patient

In the side room, Dad is the patient. Outside in the corridor, we have to be patient. The hospital is full of patients. Sometimes the patients have to wait to see a doctor (just like Dad did) and so they have to show a great deal of patience. Patients and patience are homophones. That means they sound exactly the same when we say them but they mean different things. Mr French taught us about homophones by using this example: *'They're* hanging *their* coats over *there.'* When we get back to school I might suggest to Mr French that he uses the following: 'The hospital is full of patients. They're hanging their coats over there with great patience.'

Q is for Question Mark

As we sat and waited, I thought about my room and what a dreadful state it was now in. Mostly, I was thinking about my Valentine's Day card.

The last time I'd seen it, it was on the floor in the rubble. I hadn't had time to rescue it and give it a wipe in all the rush and commotion to get Dad to the hospital.

On February 14th I'd found the card in my bag as I was putting my folder away at the end of school. It was just a plain white envelope with my name written in block capitals on the front. I knew what it must be – at least I hoped I knew what it must be and that's why I hadn't wanted to open it immediately. I wanted to keep on not knowing, to put off finding out what was inside for as long as possible.

I couldn't wait very long, to be honest. As soon as I got home I raced up to my room and tore open the envelope. On the front of the card was a big red heart and the words 'Be my Valentine' and inside was a big question mark written with a marker pen like this:

It wasn't a lot to go on.

But as I sat there in the hospital a new and interesting idea sprang into my mind. What if the question mark wasn't actually a question mark? Obviously it *was* a question mark – I'd looked at it nearly every day since February – but what if it also had another meaning. It could be a piece of punctuation and it could also be a statement. A statement that said, 'Question Mark,' as in, 'ask Mark a question'.

Wow! The more I thought about this the more it made sense and there were lots of questions I'd like to ask Mark.

It had to be Mark, didn't it? The only other person I could imagine sending me a

Valentine's Day card was Colin Timkins and that didn't bear thinking about.

Mum went off to check on Dad, leaving me alone on the bench in the corridor. After a few minutes, Finn screeched to a halt in the wheelchair and came and sat down next to me.

'Worried?' he asked.

'No,' I said.

'You look worried.'

'I'm not worried. At least not about Dad's foot.'

'My Venus flytrap,' he said, 'I know it's been playing on your mind because you can't work it out.'

'Go on then,' I said, intrigued, 'how do you get it to grow so well?'

'I keep a stash of dead flies in my desk,' he said, as if keeping a stash of dead flies in your desk was the most normal thing in the world. 'I collect them from windowsills and spiders' webs in the summer and store them in an old jam jar. I feed the dead flies to Venus all through the winter. No tap water either. Only rainwater will do. That's it.'

I was horrified and impressed at the same time. Finn was too smart for his own good.

'Why are you telling me this?' I asked.

'Because you look worried.'

'I'm not worried.'

'You really look worried.'

'I'm really not,' I said again. 'Why have you got pins stuck in your map of the world?'

'No way; I'm not telling you that. I'm trying to make you feel better but don't push it.'

'I'm *not* worried!'

'Then my work here is done.'

He returned to the wheelchair and his handbrake turns.

R is for Receiving

Mum came back to the bench and said, 'He's still receiving treatment.' I wonder if Dad thinks it's better to give or receive at the moment.

S is for Sprain (not a)

We heard Dad before we saw him. He was click, clack clacking down the long corridor on crutches, the bottom of his right leg neatly encased in pure, snow white plaster.

'It's a broken ankle,' he said sadly. 'I'm going to be in this thing for at least six weeks.'

Mum drove us home in silence.

T is for Tip

We got Dad settled in the lounge with a cup of tea and a stool to rest his foot on. He said 'Thanks' as he stared at the bare Christmas tree sitting in the soil-filled bucket in the corner of the room.

Upstairs, Mum looked at my room and said it was a tip. 'Tip' was the word that Mum and Dad always used for something that was untidy.

In the olden days, when people had rubbish that wouldn't fit in the bin they'd take it to the tip. Today, when we have rubbish that won't fit in the bin we take it to the Council's Household Waste Recovery and Recycling Centre. Mum and Dad still call it the tip, though.

This was the first time Mum had ever described my room as a tip. Finn's room, on the other hand, was always a tip. Mum said that getting Finn to tidy his room was like trying to herd cats. I imagine herding cats must be very difficult because Mum can never get Finn to keep his room tidy.

U is for Understatement

Although Mum was right when she called my room a tip, it was also an understatement. My room was a bombsite and as far away from neatly ordered and arranged as it was possible to be (I think this is what Mr French might call irony).

Fragments of plasterboard from the ceiling lay all over the floor together with thin wooden strips and various other piles of debris. Dust was everywhere.

Mum said, 'I think you'd better sleep in Finn's room tonight.'

And then she saw the horrified look on my face and said, 'Or we could get this all cleaned up now.'

I nodded eagerly.

We filled thick black bags with the bits of plaster and wood, I dusted and Mum went over and over the floor with the vacuum cleaner. I cleaned up my Valentine's Day card and put it back on my desk where it belonged. Soon my room was looking as good as new.

Apart from the huge gaping hole in my ceiling.

We were changing the sheets and pillow cases on my bed when we heard a click, clack, clacking noise on the landing. It was a sound we would get used to over the next few weeks.

Dad poked his head round the door, smiled, looked directly at Mum and said, 'Sorry.'

It was a strange sort of sorry.

It wasn't this sort of sorry:

'Sorry for crashing through the ceiling.'

And it wasn't this sort of sorry:

'Sorry that we had to spend most of the day at the hospital.'

And it certainly wasn't this sort of sorry:

'Sorry that we haven't found the decorations yet.'

It was just a 'Sorry' that was all on its own like a small boy separated from his mum in a large supermarket (sorry!). It was a permanent 'Sorry', too. It hung there in the air between Mum and Dad like a helium balloon tied around the index finger of that lost boy in the supermarket (I'll stop now, I promise).

And it was clearly full of meaning.

Mum smiled back at Dad and nodded. A tear began to well up in her eye. She quickly wiped it away and said, 'Dear me, the dust in here. It's making my eyes water.'

But it wasn't the dust. All the dust was in the vacuum cleaner.

V is for Virgo and Daughters

That was the name of the removal firm who moved us into our nice new house in January. I remember the name because it was so unusual - both the 'Virgo' bit and the 'Daughters' bit. Even though their lorry was huge, I thought there was no way they would be able to get everything from our old house into the back of it. But they did. Beds, chairs, wardrobes, washing machine, boxes, sofa. Everything. Mr Virgo and his two daughters – Jo and Sam, short for Joanna and Samantha - were highly skilled at loading up their lorry. Everything got on and the move went well.

At least that is what we all thought at the time. Dad now has a theory that Mr Virgo and his daughters didn't quite remember to carry everything off the back of the lorry (it was January and it was dark by the time they had finished). There was, he thought, one large box that must have been left on the back of the removal van.

And that was the box that contained our Christmas decorations.

So we all sat in the lounge and looked at the bare tree until Mum said, 'Well, it's too late to do anything about it now. All the shops are closed. And anyway, it doesn't matter. What matters is that we'll all be together.'

'All together with *your* family,' said Dad.

Mum started to raise an eyebrow when Dad quickly added:

'Which'll be lovely!'

He actually sounded like he meant it.

W is for World's Best Roast Potatoes

According to Dad, he makes the world's best roast potatoes. They are always cracklingly crunchy on the outside and super fluffy on the inside.

As my Christmas present to you, here is *exactly* how Dad makes his roast potatoes:

1) Buy the right potatoes. The right potatoes in this case are King Edward potatoes. No other potatoes will do (especially not Maris Pipers).

2) Try to buy good sized King Edward potatoes. The smaller ones don't work as well, apparently.

3) Peel and halve the potatoes.

4) Place the potatoes in a large pan, cover with water and add a little bit of salt. Put the lid on the pan and bring to the boil. Boil the potatoes in the water for 8 minutes (not a second more and not a second less).

5) While this is happening, put a good dollop of goose fat (not duck fat, not lard, not any other type of fat – at

all) into a roasting tin and then put the roasting tin in the oven (pre-heated to 180°C) to heat up.

6)   Drain the potatoes, put the lid back on the pan and then give the pan a really good shake. And then another shake. And then another. This will fluff up the outsides of the potatoes and help them to get super crispy.

7)   Use oven gloves to take the hot roasting tin out of the oven and then carefully, very carefully (scorching hot fat alert) use a spoon to place the potatoes gently into the fat in the roasting tin.

8)   Then you need a baster. A baster is like a bigger version of the pipettes we use in science class. Basically, it's a long thin pointed tube with a round rubbery ball at one end. You squeeze the rubbery ball, dip the pointy end in the goose fat (the *extremely* hot goose fat) and then gently release your grip on the ball. This sucks the fat up into the tube. When the tube is full of goose fat press on the

rubbery ball again to squirt the fat all over the potatoes. They all need a good coating. This is called basting.

9)   Put them into the oven and leave them there for half an hour.

10)   After half an hour, take them out, turn them over in the tin (just give them a good muddle about) and then repeat step 8.

11)   Back in the oven for another half an hour.

12)   And they're done. They'll be golden and crisp on the outside and lovely and fluffy on the inside (guaranteed). Don't worry if other things aren't ready. You can turn the oven temperature down a bit and leave the potatoes in there. They'll get a little darker in colour but they'll still be great. If you start the whole process one and a half hours before you plan to eat then everything will work out well.

X is for X-ray

Luckily for the purposes of my neatly ordered and arranged Christmas alphabet, Dad had an x-ray at the hospital. I only know three words that begin with X: x-ray, Xmas and xylophone and Mum doesn't like us using the word Xmas because she thinks it's modern and lazy. It's actually not – people have been using it for years and years (I looked it up) but if Mum doesn't like it I'm happy not to use it.

I suppose I could have put 'X is for Xylophone' and written that I really, really hope I get a xylophone for Christmas, but I didn't want a xylophone for Christmas. At First School I was put in charge of the xylophone at one our nativity plays. Xylophones are shrill, bingy-bongy things and it's all too easy to hit the wrong note (as I discovered). I certainly don't want one of my own.

Look, the letter X takes up just two pages in my dictionary - page 1755 and page 1756 – it's not a lot to go on.

Y is for Yes

That's what Mr Oddy said when Mum popped round just after we'd finished tidying my room to invite him for Christmas lunch. Mr Oddy doesn't really have any family so, with his wife gone, he would have been all alone which wouldn't have been very nice. Mum said it was The Right Thing To Do. It was the right thing to do, too.

It'll be a bit of squeeze around the table, though.

Z is for Zebra

On Christmas Eve night, I dreamed about zebras (phew!). Or rather, I dreamed about one particular zebra that had an injured ankle. He was hobbling around the plains of Africa with a plaster cast over one of his feet – just like Dad.

Not that Dad was hobbling around Africa, of course. He was hobbling around our house. I could hear him click, clack, clacking when I woke on Christmas morning; I think it might take him some time to get the hang of his crutches.

Finn was already in the lounge in his pyjamas and dressing gown opening his presents when I got down there. Our presents were in black plastic bin bags this year under the still bare tree. Our bright red Santa sacks, which we'd had since we were very small, had been stored away with the Christmas decorations, as they were every year. I was actually quite happy about the substitute bin bags. Our

Santa sacks always smelled old and musty because they spent most of the year in the attic (not this year, though).

Finn got the Mega Laser Blaster Gun thing so he was happy. I got some heavy watercolour paper and a watercolour set (fab!), some books (great!) including a new dictionary (still very few entries for the letter X...) and some new stationery (even better!).

Mum and Dad were sitting on the sofa watching the two of us and when I turned to thank them I saw that they were holding hands and crying. Not bad crying, though. This was good crying.

Wiping a tear from his eye, Dad reached behind him and produced one more beautifully wrapped present. It was rectangular in shape and tied with a bright gold bow. He held it out for me and said, 'One more present for you, Emmabella.'

I thanked them again. 'Can I save this one for later?' I asked.

'Of course,' said Mum.

'It's your present to do with as you wish,' said Dad.

So I took that last gift up to my room and carefully placed it on my bed. I didn't want to open it then, on Christmas morning; I wanted the feeling of not knowing to carry on. I wanted to put off the finding out bit; I wanted to delay the discovery of what was inside for as long as possible.

Back downstairs, Dad was in a grump. He had suddenly realised that, due to his fall and the cast on his leg, he was going to need some help with Christmas lunch. But it wasn't the proper gloomy grumpy grump he'd been in for most of the year. This was more playful and it involved laughter. Lots of laughter.

Take this, for example:

Dad declared that since he wouldn't be able to cook, Mum, Finn and I should do all the work under his supervision; he would still be in charge. Mum gave me a secret wink. It was a wink that said, 'That's what he thinks'. I laughed and

Mum laughed too as she carefully lifted the turkey out of the fridge.

It was then that Dad said:

'Look at that beautiful bird,' he paused before adding, 'and the turkey's not bad, either!'

He laughed so loud and so long at this that I wondered if he'd already been at the sweet sherry.

There was definitely something odd in the air today.

'Right,' said Dad, having finally pulled himself together, 'A kitchen is a very dangerous place. It is full of sharp knives that can cut you and hot liquids that can burn you. You must be careful.'

I think Finn spoke for all of us when he turned his sarcasm dial up to ten and said, 'Wow! Thanks, Dad. Where would we be without you?'

'Look,' replied Dad firmly, but without any trace of anger, 'I think one injury this Christmas is more than enough.'

And on that we could all agree.

Finn was put in charge of (irony alert) carrots and sprouts and I was in charge of roast potatoes (see 'W' above). I say 'in charge' but crutches or no crutches, Dad was determined to show that he was directing everything. On the whole, we ignored him and got on with our various tasks.

Mum and Dad were acting in a strange way. Not a 'bad' strange way, a 'strange' strange way. They were giggling and sniggering and talking in a way I hadn't seen them talk all year. In fact, they were talking in a way I'd never seen them talk before. There then followed whispering and more giggling. Then more sniggering and winking. And then more giggling.

It was all a bit embarrassing but as I secretly watched them enjoying each other's company I couldn't stop myself from smiling. I thought back to how worried I'd been and how, on at least two occasions, I'd had the chance to talk to Mum and Dad (separately) about how I'd been feeling.

In August, a few days after I'd discovered that I hadn't got a place on Mr

Coe's writing course Dad came into my room and sat beside me on my bed.

'We're worried about you,' he said.

'Why?' I asked.

'Because you've been so quiet. That's not like you.'

I actually think it was like me but he was right, I had been more quiet than usual. I had been quiet because I was upset and I was upset because I hadn't got a place on the writing course and I was worried about him and Mum.

I didn't say any of this to Dad, though. Saying something would only have made a bigger issue of it and I thought he probably had enough to think about.

So I stayed silent. Dad, however, seemed keen to carry on talking.

'How's school?' he asked.

'School's fine, Dad. I'm enjoying it.'

'That's good,' he said. 'I bet you're the only Emmabella there.'

'I'm definitely the only Emmabella in school.' He laughed and then I asked:

'Why did you call me Emmabella?'

'Because it's a lovely name.'

'Mum says it's an old family name.'

'It is. But that's not the reason I named you Emmabella. It means something.'

'What?' I asked.

'Well,' he said, as he stared at my bookshelves, 'Emma means 'the whole thing', or 'everything', if you like. And Bella means 'beautiful'. Your mum and I had wanted a baby for a long time and then, eventually, we had you. That meant and will always mean everything to us. You were beautiful then and it goes without saying that you're beautiful now. So there we are. Emma. Bella.'

This was all news to me. Tears began to well up in my eyes so I looked away from him and said, 'I didn't know my name meant anything.'

'Everything means something, Emmabella.'

'What about your name?' I asked, still staring at the wall behind my bed.

'Harvey? Harvey means 'eager for battle'. Grrrr!'

He actually made a sound like a lion. I think he might have been trying to cheer me up.

I turned back to Dad, 'And Mum's?'

'Well,' he said, 'that's an easy one. I think you can work out what Angelica means.'

He was right. I could.

I was going to ask him what 'Fionton' meant but at the mention of Mum's name he seemed to drift off into his own thoughts. After a moment he came to, looked at me and said, 'As long as you're okay.'

With that, he stood up and was gone.

A couple of weeks after that, I was sitting on my bed flicking through my dictionary when Mum came in to see me. She had also noticed that I'd been quiet but by then I was also frustrated.

For a few weeks I'd been working on a still life drawing at Art Club and I just couldn't get it right. Mr Wise had arranged a pair of old walking boots on a table in the middle of the group and asked us all to draw them. I couldn't get my drawing just as I wanted it so I kept scrunching up my efforts and starting again. Everyone else had moved on to portraits but I, cross with myself for not being able to get it right, was still asking Mr Wise to set up the old boots on the table every week.

I told Mum.

'You'll get there,' she said.

'What if I don't? What if I can't get it right?'

'Emma,' she said, firmly, 'I want you to stop feeling sorry for yourself.'

'Why?'

'Because it's a waste of energy. Never forget what you have,' she paused and looked straight into my eyes, 'and never forget what you made.'

'I've never made anything,' I replied, grumpily.

'Emma,' she said, quietly, 'you made the most important thing in the world. Before you came along, your father and I were a couple. And then you were born and you made us a family.'

I started to cry and Mum put her arm around my shoulder and kissed me on the side of my head.

'Never forget that. Never forget what you made.'

'What about Finn?' I asked as I wiped salty tears off my cheeks with my sleeve.

'Finn,' she thought about this for a moment, 'Finn completed the family. That's what he did. But never mind Finn, he's fine. It's you I'm worried about.'

And there was my chance. With my cheeks hot and my mum's arm around me, that was the moment to say, 'And I'm really worried about you and Dad, too.'

But I didn't.

On Christmas morning, as I craftily watched Dad make Mum laugh again, I was glad that I hadn't said anything. It had clearly been a sensitive situation and if I'd said something it might have made things worse. I don't know what the problem was and I don't want to know. Just like Grandpa said, there are some things we are not meant to know.

I had almost finished peeling the potatoes when the doorbell rang and Nana and Grandpa Grundy and Auntie Maisie and Uncle Dougie came bustling in. Greetings were exchanged and there were more presents for me and Finn – action figures for him and a diary and more stationery for me (yippee!).

The new arrivals soon spotted Dad's crutches and were, naturally, keen to hear what had happened. 'I fell through the attic onto Emmabella's floor,' was Dad's limited response.

They all reacted to this.

There was sympathy from Auntie Maisie as she threw her arms around him, crutches and all, and whimpered, 'You poor, poor thing.'

There was advice from Grandpa Grundy, 'When you're in an attic, Harvey, you need to stay on the beams.'

Nana Grundy was indifferent to Dad's injury. 'Never mind his foot,' she whispered, as she leaned over to me, 'how's your bedroom?'

Uncle Dougie tried, and failed, to stifle a giggle. By way of a reply, Dad shot him a look (withering with menaces).

Uncle Dougie then did what he always does when he visits our house. He had a good look around the lounge and the dining room to see if we had bought a new TV (we hadn't), a new DVD player (no) or a new hi-fi system (nope!). He soon returned from his search and said, 'I like what you've done with the Christmas tree!'

Uncle Dougie was being sarcastic, I think, because we hadn't done anything with the tree so there was nothing to like. Anyway, Dad was straight on the case:

'Dougie, would you pitch in and help with lunch? We're a bit short-handed what with me being on crutches.'

'Roger to that,' said Uncle Dougie. 'I am something of an expert in all things culinary. Just bought myself a new set of knives, actually. Had them imported – all the way from Japan. They're not razor sharp, they're laser sharp!'

'That sounds great, Dougie,' said Dad, 'Now, you see that bag of onions over there? Perhaps you could slice them thinly for me?'

'What? All of them?' asked Dougie.

'That's right,' said Dad.

'Okay,' said a puzzled-looking Dougie.

Mum was looking puzzled, too. She'd had a strange look on her face throughout Dad and Dougie's conversation. It was a look that said, 'Why are you asking Dougie to thinly slice a bag of onions?'

Dad saw the look and said, 'I thought we'd have onion soup for a starter...'

This clearly came as news to Mum who shook her head and had another sip of sweet sherry.

Slicing onions certainly kept Uncle Dougie quiet. It also made him cry and smell of onions for the rest of the day.

'I love your tree,' Aunt Maisie said to Mum after she'd returned from her own exploration of our house.

'Do you?' asked Mum, finding something new to be puzzled about.

It appeared that Aunt Maisie was being sincere. 'I really, really love your tree. It's such a bold statement,' she said as she tightly clasped Mum's arm.

'Is it?' asked Mum, still clearly puzzled.

'It is,' said Auntie Maisie seriously, 'ignoring society's expectation of embellishment and decoration. Just allowing the tree to speak for itself. Allowing the tree to be... a tree.'

Mum stared at Maisie, her mouth open in astonishment.

'You're very brave,' continued Maisie, 'very brave and very bold.'

Auntie Maisie started to cry. Perhaps it was the onions.

I was on stage 10 of the all-important roast potato preparation schedule (turning and basting if you've forgotten the recipe – which you shouldn't – it's really good) when Nana Grundy silently glided over to see what I was doing. She was as thin as a rake, Nana Grundy – 'I lived through a war, my girl, no chance of getting fat then' – and had the ability to move around a room without making a sound as a result.

She arrived just in time to see me basting the potatoes with the baster.

'What do you call that?'

'This, Nana, is a baster. You use it for basting the potatoes with the goose fat.'

'Ach!' she said.

'Ach!' (always with an exclamation mark) was one of Nana Grundy's favourite expressions. It could have a variety of meanings depending on the situation.

'Have you not heard of a spoon?' she asked.

'Dad says this is better.'

'Your dad says a lot of things.'

This meant, 'Your dad says a lot of things and a lot of them are rubbish.'

I felt I should stick up for Dad (and his baster) particularly as he had a broken ankle, so I said:

'It seems to be working very well-'

'Pah!' said Nana. This was another of Nana's favourite expressions and it was almost always followed by:

'It's the devil's work, Emmabella, the devil's work.'

Luckily, Mr Oddy arrived from next door which quickly put an end to our basterbased conversation. He had a bottle of wine in one hand and a kettle in the other.

'My small contribution to the day,' he said, as he handed the bottle of wine to Mum.

Mum thanked him and pointed at the kettle. 'Is that for us, too?' she asked.

'No!' said Mr Oddy, a little sharply. 'This is mine. Mine! It is my Christmas present to myself.' For good measure he added, 'I will not let this kettle out of my sight.'

'Okay,' said Mum, as she took a small step backwards.

From the other side of the kitchen, Nana Grundy gave Mum a look that said, 'Who on earth is this strange man and why have you invited him for Christmas lunch?'

Mum did the introductions and then got on with the gravy.

From his long face and stooped appearance it seemed that the Christmas spirit had not yet touched Mr Oddy (although the stoop might be because he helped carry Dad down the stairs yesterday, I suppose). Mum poured him a large glass of sherry. Perhaps that would help.

Not that Mr Oddy got much of a chance to enjoy his drink.

'Right, Mr Oddy,' said Finn who clearly wanted something as he hadn't called him 'Noddy', 'time for a bit of a mega blaster laser gun challenge!' Finn had a gun in each hand. He held one out for Mr Oddy.

'With me? But I've got a sore back. Can't someone else play with you?'

''Fraid not, Mr Oddy,' said Finn. He pointed at Dad, 'He's in a cast,' he pointed at Uncle Dougie, 'he's chopping onions,' he pointed at Mum, 'she's making gravy... or something,' he pointed at me, 'she's my sister and probably has something against full-on armed combat,' he pointed at Nana Grundy, 'old,' he pointed at Grandpa Grundy, 'older,' he pointed at Auntie Maisie and actually couldn't find the words to describe why she was not cut out for a mega blaster challenge, before swivelling back round to face Mr Oddy again, 'it's definitely got to be you.'

So Mr Oddy took a big swig of his sherry, asked me to watch his kettle for him and got strapped into a mega blaster breastplate. After Finn got into his breastplate, blaster guns were chosen (red for Finn, blue for Mr Oddy) and rules of engagement were agreed (just like Art Club, there were no rules). Then off they went through the house, Finn and Mr Oddy, blasting and dodging blasts as they went.

Grandpa Grundy nodded his head for me to join him in the hall. 'I see the ice floes appear to have melted in the situation you were so worried about,' he said when we were alone.

'I know,' I said, 'I've never seen them like this. They're getting on really well.'

'First rate, first rate. You see? I told you everything would work out for the best.'

'Dad said sorry.'

'Sometimes that is all that is needed to take the wind out of the sails. It can take a big man to say sorry. But as long as you're happy, that's what matters.'

I nodded to show that I really was happy.

'No more worries?' asked Grandpa.

'None at all.'

'Excellent. I can smell turkey. Come on.'

I followed him back into the kitchen.

Lunch was nearly ready. The turkey was out of the oven and resting, the potatoes were just short of golden perfection and the vegetables were boiling and steaming away on the cooker. And I was watching Mr Oddy's kettle.

'Sorry, Dougie,' said Dad as Dougie continued to work his way through all the onions. 'It looks like everything else is ready. I think we'd better forget the soup.' That'd teach Dougie to laugh at Dad's accident.

Dougie opened his mouth to protest just as we all heard an agonising 'Yelp!' from the hall. And then we saw Finn hobbling into the kitchen supported by Mr Oddy.

Apparently, and much to everyone's surprise, Mr Oddy had taken to the mega blaster gun battle with enthusiasm. So much enthusiasm, in fact, that he had charged down the stairs, leapt off from the fourth stair up, cried 'Geronimo!' and collided with a crunching thud into Finn who had decided, at that very moment, to stealthily pounce from the lounge doorway in a surprise counter-attack of his own.

Mr Oddy had landed squarely on Finn's right foot which had caused the yelp we had all heard. Luckily, it didn't result in us having to spend the rest of the day in the hospital. It was only a bruise (quite a dark and vivid blue bruise, actually) and it made Finn cry (the big baby).

'Thanks for the battle anyway, Noddy,' said Finn after the tears had finally dried up.

There was no 'Noddy' reaction from Mr Oddy. In fact, the two of them shook hands and Mr Oddy said, 'It was a pleasure, Finn, a pleasure. Perhaps after lunch, if your foot's better, we can have another go?'

Finn nodded eagerly.

Everyone was around the table (it was a squeeze) as I carried in the roast potatoes (a personal triumph even if I say so myself. There was an approving nod from Dad) followed by Mum carrying the now bronzed and fragrant turkey.

'Mr Oddy,' said Mum, 'would you mind moving your kettle off the table so I can put this down?'

Mr Oddy did as he was asked but kept half an eye on his kettle throughout the meal.

There were happy murmurings from everyone as Mum began to carve at 1:30pm on the dot, the exact time she had said lunch would be ready.

This was the first time in her married life that Mum had got to carve the turkey. I began to wonder if Dad was milking the old 'I'm disabled' thing a bit. I'm sure he could have leaned against the table and carved or even done it sitting down. In any event, Mum seemed to enjoy having a large fork and a very sharp knife in her hands and soon we were all tucking in.

Uncle Dougie had brought the Christmas crackers as his contribution to the day (probably imported from somewhere). I got a curved metal object which Mum said was a shoehorn. Uncle Dougie said it was sterling silver. It'll probably come in handy for something although I'm not sure what. Finn got a small pointed thing which Dougie said was a decorative stopper for a wine bottle. This was also sterling silver. Dougie got an over-sized sterling silver paperclip and offered to swap with Finn (Dougie really wanted the wine stopper). The stopper was conical with a sharply pointed end and it was very heavy for such a small object. I think Finn could see its potential as a weapon of some sort so he said no. I really liked the look of the over-sized paperclip but Dougie didn't offer to swap with me (and who can blame him?) so I was stuck with the shoehorn. Mum got a sterling silver beer bottle opener (she doesn't drink beer); Nana Grundy got a small sterling silver picture frame (just big enough for a passport photo – so that'll come in handy if she ever decides to display her passport photo on the mantelpiece); Auntie Maisie got a tiny set of playing cards (she doesn't play cards); Mr Oddy got three wooden golf tees (he doesn't play golf, as far as I know) and Dad got toe nail clippers (loser!).

As everyone greedily gobbled down the food, Nana Grundy turned to Mr Oddy and said, 'Why do you walk around with an electric kettle?'

Mr Oddy smiled a funny little smile and said, 'I know. It's silly really. It all started in January...'

And so Mr Oddy told us all about his year.

Mrs Oddy left Mr Oddy on the same day that we moved here in January. We – Mum, Dad, Finn and I – knew this because we'd seen it happen. We pulled up outside with Mr Virgo's removal lorry following behind, jumped out of the car excited to be at our new house only to find Mrs Oddy (as it turned out to be) storming out of the house next door. She gave us all a furious look, climbed into her car and sped off. A moment later, the door opened again, a suitcase came flying out and Mr Oddy (as it turned out to be) shouted, 'And don't come back!'

This, it seemed to me at the time, was the very definition of closing the door after the horse had bolted. Not that Mrs Oddy was a horse, of course and the door was open and not closed. What I mean is that Mr Oddy's clear desire to have the last word had backfired. Mrs Oddy was gone; the only people to witness the 'last word' were us four and Mr Virgo and his two daughters.

Obviously, us moving in and Mrs Oddy moving out were not connected (even though Mrs Bottomley, our Geography teacher, once told us that everything actually is connected. She said that if a butterfly flaps its wings in Tokyo it can cause a hurricane in California. Mark Dangerfield bravely, boldly and magnificently asked Mrs Bottomley how big the butterflies were in Tokyo). Anyway, Mr and Mrs Oddy's little drama certainly made for an interesting introduction to Cherry Tree Terrace.

Mr Oddy continued his tale of woe.

Mrs Oddy had left him for a photocopier salesman called Steve from Ashby-de-la-

Zouch she'd met at a conference in Wolverhampton. Mr Oddy said that the rest of the year had been taken up with him and Mrs Oddy arguing (via email and text message) about who owned what; which books belonged to Mrs Oddy and which to Mr Oddy; which CDs were his and which were hers, and so on. A couple of weeks ago, he said, he'd had enough of the constant 'back and forth bartering and bickering' (his phrase and one I like and will pinch for my own future use) so he phoned her up told her that on a particular afternoon he would be out and she could come round and collect everything that was hers. He returned home on the evening of the appointed day to find that Mrs Oddy had taken all the books, all the CDs and all the pictures.

She'd also taken the kettle.

At this, the table was silent. Even Uncle Dougie couldn't think of anything smart to say in response. He just tutted and shook his head.

Mr Oddy had a little cry. Auntie Maisie, sitting next to him, also began to cry.

Then she grasped his hand and said, 'You poor, poor man. That is the saddest story I have ever heard. *Ever* heard. But you must be brave. Brave and strong.'

I'm not sure if it was Auntie Maisie's words but Mr Oddy seemed to brighten up a bit. And then he started laughing.

And then he couldn't stop laughing.

We all looked at him cautiously; perhaps in the way a bomb disposal expert looks at a bomb. This was unexpected. Mum and I shared a look that said, 'What's happening..?' But then Mr Oddy stopped laughing and said:

'Do you know what the funny thing is?'

We all shook our heads nervously because we had absolutely no idea what the funny thing was.

'The funny thing is,' continued Mr Oddy, 'that you don't know what her first name is!'

We all nodded. None of us knew her first name.

'And do you know what the even funnier thing is?'

We all shook our heads again at exactly the same time just like the synchronized swimmers you see at the Olympics.

'The even funnier thing is that you don't know what her second name is.'

Mum shot me a worried look. It was a look that said, 'Where on earth is he going with this?' I returned Mum's look with a look of my own. My look said, 'I haven't got a clue.'

'Well,' said Mr Oddy, now shaking uncontrollably with laughter, 'her first name is Susan and...' there was a slight pause at this point. It wasn't for dramatic effect, it was because Mr Oddy was laughing so hard that he could barely get the words out, '...and her second name is Helen.' He was now laughing so much that he almost fell off his chair.

We weren't laughing. At least not to begin with.

Dad, who likes crosswords and messing around with words (and who was, after all, the first to make the Nigel Oddy equals 'Noddy' connection) was the first to get it. He started with a low chuckle which grew louder and louder just as Mr Oddy's laughter was becoming more 'inside voice' as Mum might say.

'Don't you see?' said Mr Oddy, 'Susan Helen Oddy. S. H. Oddy. Shoddy!'

We all got this and we all started laughing. All except for Finn who didn't get it.

'What does that mean?' he asked.

'Well, young Finn,' said Mr Oddy, stifling his amusement for a moment, 'Shoddy means something that is of poor quality - not fit for purpose. And that is exactly what she turned out to be!'

We all laughed again, including Finn this time.

Just as the hilarity was subsiding, Grandpa Grundy who had, up to that point, spent the lunch quietly eating and sipping on a glass of rum decided to speak.

'I can see why she decided to leave you!' he said.

There was a momentary pause as we didn't quite know how Mr Oddy would take this but he started giggling again and so did the rest of us.

After pudding we tidied up the lunch things and sat down to watch the Queen. Or rather, we all sat down for a minute and then the National Anthem piped up and this got Grandpa Grundy on his feet so we all stood up, too. Then we all sat down again.

The Queen talked about the importance of families and the importance of tradition (I think she always does).

Anyway, all Her Majesty's talk of tradition and family struck a nerve with Nana Grundy who was soon sobbing away as the Queen spoke. Grandpa Grundy took her hand and then started crying, too.

What was happening today?

The Queen done and all tears wiped away, Finn and Mr Oddy decided to embark on another epic mega blaster gun challenge. At various points in the afternoon we could hear odd snippets of battle cries from far off places in the house. Things like:

'Stay right where you are, Noddy. You're toast!'

And:

'Say hello to my little friend!'

In the lounge, Grandpa was holding Nana's hand as she began to doze on the sofa.

'Do you want to play Monopoly, Dad?' whispered Mum.

'Not on your nelly,' Grandpa replied.

'Oh come on,' said Mum, 'we'd really like you to play.'

'Well,' said Grandpa, 'tough titties!'

Naughty Grandpa! No more rum for him.

The rest of us gathered around the table, moved Mr Oddy's kettle on to one of the chairs and set up the Monopoly board.

Uncle Dougie likes to think he is an expert at Monopoly and always wins. I like to think this makes for a boring game so this year I have been practising a few techniques of my own.

The autumn half term was wet and cold so Penny, Molly and I spent a lot of the week playing Monopoly (at my suggestion and urging). They both got into it eventually and I discovered a technique that enabled me to win more often than not.

It's quite simple really. Buy everything you can (apart from the stations and the utilities – they're rubbish) as quickly as you can. This puts you in a strong position because you'll be able to choose who to trade with in order to get a full set of properties.

That was what I did on Christmas Day. Naturally, I decided not to trade with Uncle Dougie which prevented him from building houses and hotels on any of his properties. He couldn't even get all four stations (his back-up plan, I think) because I bought Fenchurch Street when I saw what he was up to.

I was happy to trade with everyone else, though. After the first few rounds I had Northumberland Avenue and Whitehall which meant I only needed Pall Mall for the full set. Auntie Maisie swapped her Pall Mall for my Pentonville Road so I easily ended up with the three locations I needed to start building. Uncle Dougie gave Auntie Maisie a look that said, 'What on earth are you doing?'

After a few more trips around the board my pile of cash was growing steadily so I decided to develop my game further. Mum agreed to give me Vine Street and Marlborough Street in exchange for Mayfair. Uncle Dougie gave Mum a look that said 'Are you quite mad?'

I now had every property between Jail and Free Parking (except for Electric Company and Marylebone Station, they're rubbish remember) and enough cash to put houses and hotels on each of them. It was only a matter of time.

Uncle Dougie grew more and more frustrated.

'This really isn't fair,' he declared at one point.

'This is Monopoly,' I replied. 'It isn't meant to be fair.'

'Look,' he said, 'I'll give you Trafalgar Square and The Angel Islington. All I want is Bond Street.'

'I want doesn't get,' I said with a smile.

'Trafalgar Square, The Angel Islington *and* Piccadilly,' was his counter offer.

I considered for a moment. 'I think not,' I replied.

It was obvious that Uncle Dougie was getting angrier because his voice was getting higher and his face was turning redder. It was Auntie's Maisie's turn to give someone a look. Her look was directed straight at Dougie and it said, 'Behave yourself!'

He didn't behave himself, though. He ignored Auntie Maisie and yelled, 'It's a bloody game! What do you bloody want?'

'What I want,' I replied very calmly, 'is to see you penniless, property-less and ground into the dirt begging for mercy.'

At least no one could accuse me of not getting into the spirit of the game.

I won, of course, but it took a lot longer than I had expected. Auntie Maisie was the first to go bankrupt, followed by Dad (who hadn't really been taking it seriously – he'd spent the entire game making gooey-gooey eyes at Mum and saying Chesty Community instead of Community

Chest); Mum finished a good third. Uncle Dougie was the last to go out. He may be a lot of things but he's certainly persistent.

Uncle Dougie spent the rest of the evening huffing and puffing and saying it wasn't fair. Eventually, the shame of defeat got too much for him and he said to Auntie Maisie that it was time to go. They quickly bundled Nana and Grandpa into the back of their new car and were off into the night.

Mr Oddy cheerfully thanked Mum and Dad for what he described as a wonderful day, shook Finn's hand and arranged a follow-up mega blaster gun battle before wobbling a little unevenly, kettle in hand, back next door.

In the lounge, Mum and Dad were curled up in each other's arms, not talking, but both smiling. Finn and I looked at each other and decided it was time for us to go to bed.

Finn skipped merrily up the stairs ahead of me, his two mega blaster guns in his hands. He'd got what he wanted for Christmas and he was happy. As I wearily followed him up the stairs I thought about Mum and Dad on the sofa and I realised that I'd got exactly what I'd wished for, too.

Mum and Dad were talking and everything was back to how it should be.

It had been an odd day. Everyone had cried at least once – everyone except me, I should say – but despite this it had been a very happy day and I hoped, hoped, hoped that it was going to last.

The busyness of the day had made me forget all about the huge gaping hole in my bedroom ceiling but it was still there looming above my head, like the mouth of some giant monster just waiting to gobble me up, when I got back in my room. There was no chance of getting the hole fixed before the new year so I would just have to get used to it.

I'd also forgotten about my last Christmas present, the neatly wrapped rectangular gift that Mum and Dad had given me in the morning. There it was just sitting on my bed waiting to be opened.

I untied the bow, slid my finger under the edge of the wrapping paper and carefully prised the sellotape away. For some reason, I didn't want to just rip the paper off. Something about this last, final present meant that it deserved a little bit of respect. So I removed the paper slowly and deliberately without a single tear. Inside the paper was a dark green box and inside the box was...

My first ever fountain pen! Yes! Yes! Yes! It was a deep, deep red with a polished silver cap and it was the most beautiful pen I had ever seen. I took it out of the box and held it in my hand. It was far heavier than any of the pens I had ever used before and it was clearly designed for proper writing and proper storytelling.

And then I saw something else in the box. It was a small piece of notepaper neatly folded in half. I opened it up to find this:

Emmabella,

Mr Coe rang last week.

He has a spare place on his

writing course – you start

your lessons in the first week of January. We know you'll work hard and we hope that you get to live your dream.

Love

Mum and Dad

I looked down again at the note just as a single salty tear fell from my eye. It fell like a big, brilliant, wonderful man who wasn't afraid to say sorry falls onto a bedroom floor and landed with a splodge on the crisp white paper. I quickly dried it with my sleeve.

I was going to keep this note for ever.

Even though it had been a busy day and I was tired I just had to use my new pen right then. At my desk I carefully took the top off the pen and smiled as the gold nib gleamed in the light of my desk lamp. I opened a new notebook and held the pen over the clean, lined page.

Where to begin? Where to begin?

Of course!

This is the story of my Christmas.

31735317R00072

Printed in Great Britain
by Amazon